**SEFTON PUBLIC LIBRARIES**

Please return/renew this item by
the last date shown.

0 5 MAY 2016

WITHDRAWN
FROM STOCK

Renew at www.catalogue.sefton.gov.uk
or by telephone at **any** Sefton library:

Bootle: 0151 934 5781
Crosby: 0151 257 6400
Formby: 01704 874177

Meadows: 0151 288 6727
Netherton: 0151 525 0607
Southport: 0151 934 2118

0 029 681 23X

ORCHARD BOOKS
338 Euston Road, London NW1 3BH
*Orchard Books Australia*
Level 17/207 Kent Street, Sydney, NSW 2000

This text was first published in Great Britain in the form of a
gift collection called The Orchard Book of Shakespeare Stories,
illustrated by Angela Barrett in 2001
The first edition of each story first published in paperback
in Great Britain in 2003
This bind-up edition published in 2014

Text © Andrew Matthews 2001
Illustrations © Tony Ross 2002

The rights of Andrew Matthews to be identified as the author and
Tony Ross as the illustrator of this work have been asserted by them
in accordance with the Copyright, Designs, and Patents Act, 1988.

A CIP catalogue record for this book is available
from the British Library.

ISBN 978 1 40833 381 5

1 3 5 7 9 10 8 6 4 2

Printed in Great Britain

The paper and board used in this paperback are natural recyclable
products made from wood grown in sustainable forests.
The manufacturing processes conform to the environmental
regulations of the country of origin.

Orchard Books is a division of Hachette Children's Books,
an Hachette UK company

www.hachette.co.uk

# Contents

# Macbeth

# Cast List

The Three Witches – or Weird Sisters

## Macbeth

Thane of Glamis
General to King Duncan

## Lady Macbeth

Wife to Macbeth

## Banquo

General to King Duncan

## King Duncan

King of Scotland

## Malcolm and Donalbain

The King's sons

## Macduff

Thane of Fife

## A servant of Glamis Castle

## Two Murderers

## The Scene

Scotland in the eleventh century.

*When shall we three meet again?*
*In thunder, lightning, or in rain?*
*When the hurly-burly's done,*
*When the battle's lost and won.*

First and Second Witches; I.i.

# Macbeth

All day, the three witches waited on the edge of the battlefield. Hidden by mist and magic, they watched the Scottish army win a victory over the invading forces of Norway, and after the fight was done they lingered on, gloating over the moans of the dying.

As thunder rolled overhead and rain lashed down, one of the witches raised her long, hooked nose to the wind and sniffed like a dog taking a scent. "He will be here soon," she said.

The second witch stroked the tuft of silvery hair that sprouted from her chin, and grinned, showing her gums. "I hear the sound of hooves, sisters," she said.

The third witch held up a piece of rock crystal in front of her milky, blind eyes. Inside the crystal, something seemed to move. "I see him!" she screeched. "He comes! Let the spell begin."

\* \* \*

Two Scottish generals rode slowly away
from the battlefield, their heads lowered
against the driving rain.

One was Macbeth, the Thane of Glamis,
the bravest soldier in King Duncan's army.
He was tall, broad-shouldered and had a
warrior's face, broken-nosed and scarred
from old fights.

His companion and friend Banquo was younger and slimmer, with a mouth that was quick to smile, although he wasn't smiling now.

Macbeth's dark eyes were distant as he recalled the details of the day's slaughter. 'A hard fight to protect an old, feeble King,' he thought. 'If I ruled Scotland...' His mind drifted off into a familiar daydream: he saw himself seated on the throne, with the golden crown of Scotland circling his brow...

Suddenly his horse reared and whinnied, its eyes rolling in terror. Macbeth struggled to control the horse, and at that moment a bolt of lightning turned the air violet. In the eerie light he saw three weird hags barring the way, their wild hair and ragged robes streaming like tattered flags in the wind.

Macbeth's hand
flew to his sword,
but Banquo hissed
out an urgent
warning. "No, my
friend! I do not think
swords can harm creatures like these."

A small, cold fear entered Macbeth's
heart, and he snarled to conceal it.
"What do you want?" he demanded of the
witches. "Stand aside!"

Moving as one,
the witches raised
their left arms and
pointed crooked
fingers at Macbeth.
They spoke, and
their voices grated
like iron on stone.

16

*"All hail, Macbeth, Thane of Glamis!"*
*"All hail, Macbeth, Thane of Cawdor!"*
*"All hail, Macbeth, who shall be King!"*

Macbeth gave a startled gasp – how had these withered crones come to read his secret thoughts?

The witches turned their fingers to Banquo. "All hail, Banquo!" they chanted. "Your children shall be kings!"

And they vanished like a mist of breath on a mirror.

"Were they ghosts?" Banquo whispered in amazement.

"They were madwomen!" snorted Macbeth. "How can I be Thane of Cawdor? He is alive and well and one of King Duncan's most trusted friends."

"And how could my children be kings if you took the throne?" Banquo asked.

The sound of hoofbeats made both men turn their heads. Out of the rain appeared a royal herald. He pulled his horse to a halt and lifted a hand in salute. "I bring great news!" he announced. "The Thane of Cawdor has confessed to treason and has been executed. The King has given his title and lands to you, noble Macbeth. He has proclaimed you as his heir, after his sons Malcolm and Donalbain. All hail, Macbeth, Thane of Glamis *and* Cawdor!"

Macbeth's face turned deathly pale. 'So the witches told the truth?' he thought. 'Only Duncan and his sons stand between me and the crown! My wife must know of this – I will write to her tonight.'

Macbeth was so deep in thought that he didn't notice the troubled look that

Banquo gave him. The witches had left a scent of evil in the air, and Banquo seemed to smell it clinging to his friend.

\* \* \*

Lady Macbeth stood at the window of her bedchamber, gazing out at the clouds gathering above the turrets of Glamis Castle. In her right hand, she held the letter from her husband, and its words echoed through her mind. "Glamis, Cawdor, King, you could have them all!" she whispered. "But I know you too well, my lord. You want greatness, but you shrink from what you must do to get it. If only…"

There was a knock at the door. Lady Macbeth started and turned, her long black hair whispering against the green silk of her gown. "Come!" she called.

A servant entered. "A message from Lord Macbeth, my lady," he said. "He bids you prepare a royal banquet, for the King will stay at Glamis tomorrow night."

"What?" Lady Macbeth gasped in amazement. "Are you mad?" She quickly recovered herself. "Go and tell the other servants to make ready for the King!" she commanded.

When she was alone again, Lady Macbeth opened the window, and a blast of cold air caught her hair and swirled it about her face. "Fate leads Duncan to Glamis!" she murmured. "Come to me, Powers of Darkness! Fill me with cruelty, so I may teach my husband how to be ruthless!"

A low growl of thunder answered her.

✳ ✳ ✳

Macbeth rode ahead of the King's party, and arrived at Glamis just after sunrise. When his wife greeted him he noticed a hard, determined look in her eyes. "The King sleeps here tonight," he said. "Is his room ready?"

"All is ready…for Duncan's last night on Earth!" said Lady Macbeth.

"What do you mean?" Macbeth asked.

Lady Macbeth moved closer, and spoke in a low voice. "I guessed the thoughts that lay behind your letter," she said. "Duncan is old and weak. His sons are not 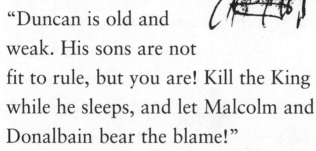 fit to rule, but you are! Kill the King while he sleeps, and let Malcolm and Donalbain bear the blame!"

Macbeth was astonished – first the witches, and now his wife had seen his innermost thoughts. Some strange force seemed to have taken control of his life, and he fought against it. "I will never commit murder and treason!" he declared.

"I will put a
sleeping-potion
in a jug of wine
and send it to
the guards at the
King's door," Lady
Macbeth said quickly.

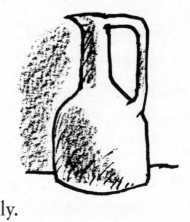

"They will sleep like babes. It will be
easy for you to slip into Duncan's room."

"No! I cannot!"
Macbeth groaned.
Lady Macbeth's
face twisted into
a sneer. "This is
your real chance
to be King," she
said. "Are you
too cowardly
to take it?"

"I am no coward!" snapped Macbeth.

"Then prove it!" Lady Macbeth hissed.
"Kill the old man and take the throne!"

Once more, the strange force moved
through Macbeth, flowing into him from
his wife until he was unable to resist. 'All
hail, Macbeth, who shall be King!' he
thought, and he could almost feel the
crown upon his head.

Long after the castle had fallen silent, Macbeth left his room and crept along the corridors. His hands trembled, and the sound of his pulse in his ears was like the beating of a battle drum. 'This is the hour of the wolf and the witch,' he thought,

'when evil spirits roam the night.'

And as the words crossed his mind, a
ghostly glow gathered in the darkness,
shaping itself into a dagger that floated
in the air, shining with a sickly green light.
Macbeth almost cried out in terror.

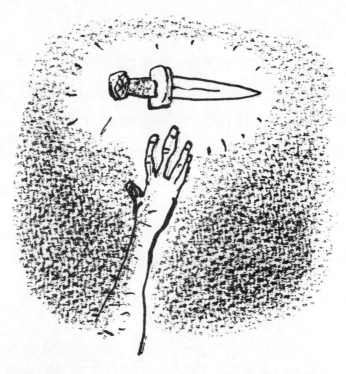

"Be calm!" he told himself. "This is a trick of the mind!" To prove it, he reached out his hand to take the dagger, but it floated away from him and pointed the way to Duncan's door. Blood began to ooze from the blade, as though the iron were weeping red tears.

A bell tolled midnight.

"Duncan's funeral bell is ringing!" muttered Macbeth, and he followed the dagger through the gloom.

Lady Macbeth also heard the bell toll, and it seemed a long time before her husband returned. There was blood on his face and hands, and he carried two daggers.

"You should not have brought the daggers here!" said Lady Macbeth. "Go back and put them into the guards' hands, as we planned!"

Macbeth's eyes were blank. He shook his head. "I will not go back there!" he said hoarsely.

"Then *I will!*" said Lady Macbeth, and snatched the daggers from Macbeth's hands and left the room.

Macbeth stood where he was, shivering uncontrollably, seeing nothing but Duncan's dead eyes staring. He tried to pray, but his lips and tongue would not form the words.

In a short while, Lady Macbeth came back, holding her red hands up to the candle-light. "I smeared blood over the guards' faces, to make them seem guilty," she said. "In the morning, we will have them tortured until they say that Duncan's sons paid them to kill him!"

Her face was so full of triumph and cruelty, that Macbeth no longer recognised it. He turned away, and caught sight of his reflection in the mirror. It was as if he were looking at someone else – as if he and his wife had become strangers to themselves and each other.

Glamis Castle was woken in the grey light of dawn by voices shouting, "Murder! The King is slain!" Shocked guests ran from their rooms and spoke in whispers. Who could have murdered the King?

Rumours flew through the castle like swallows – and suspicion fell on Malcolm and Donalbain, who had the most to gain from their father's death.

Malcolm and Donalbain were convinced that Macbeth was the murderer, but they did not dare to accuse him – who would believe that the hero of the battle against the Norwegians would slay his own King?

Though they knew it would be taken as proof of their guilt, Duncan's sons fled for their lives. Donalbain sailed for Ireland,

and Malcolm rode across the border into England, to put himself under the protection of the English King.

Now nothing stood between Macbeth and the throne.

He was crowned, but the crown did not
bring him the pleasure he had imagined.
His secret dream had come true, but he
was disturbed by other dreams – dreams
of what the witches had
foretold for Banquo's
descendants.

'Have I lied and
murdered to set
Banquo's spawn on
the throne?' he brooded.
'I must find a way to rid myself
of him, and his son.'

A dark plan formed in Macbeth's
mind, and he kept it a secret – even from
Lady Macbeth. Without either of them
realising, the strange force that had
compelled them to kill Duncan was slowly
driving them apart.

* * *

Macbeth held a coronation feast in the royal castle at Dunsinane. Many of the nobles who attended remarked that Macbeth's old friend, Banquo, was not present, but Macbeth laughed when they mentioned it.

"Lord Banquo and his son must have
been delayed on their way," he said
lightly. Only he knew what had delayed
them, for he had hired two murderers to
ambush them on the road.

At the height of the feast, a servant brought Macbeth a message that two men wished to see him on urgent business. Macbeth hurried to his private chambers, and found the murderers waiting there.

"Have you done what I paid you to do?" Macbeth demanded.

"Banquo is dead, my lord," one of the murderers said. "We cut his throat and threw the body into a ditch."

Macbeth sighed with relief – perhaps now he would sleep peacefully. But then he sensed something wrong: neither of the murderers would look at him, and they kept anxiously shuffling their feet.

"And his son?" said Macbeth.

The reply was shattering. "He escaped, my lord. Banquo's son still lives."

As he returned to the banqueting hall, doubts tortured Macbeth like scorpions' stings. 'Banquo's son still lives!' he thought. 'Lives to take his revenge on me, to claim the throne and father sons who will rule after him. Is there no end to the blood that must be shed before I find peace?'

As he entered the hall, Macbeth put on a false smile to hide his troubled mind; but the smile froze when he saw a hooded figure seated in his chair. "Who dares to sit in my place?" he roared.

The guests fell silent and looked bewildered: the King's chair was empty.

"Why...no one, my lord!" said Lady Macbeth, with a forced laugh. She could see that something was wrong with her husband, but she could not guess what. "The King is jesting!" she told the nobles.

"This is no jest!" barked Macbeth. He strode angrily towards the figure, then recoiled in horror as it drew back its hood.

For what he saw was Banquo – with weed tangled in his hair, and mud streaked across his face, with a deep gash in his neck that sent a stream of blood pattering onto the flagstones and haunting, glassy eyes that stared and stared.

"Get rid of him!" Macbeth screeched.

The nobles sprang to their feet, drawing their daggers, knocking over chairs and wine cups in the confusion.

"Back to your grave!" sobbed Macbeth.

Banquo smiled – there was blood in his mouth, and his teeth shone white through it, then he faded into the shadows and the torchlight.

"My lords, the King is ill," Lady Macbeth said desperately. "Leave us now, and let him rest. In the morning, he will be himself again."

"Myself?" Macbeth moaned softly to himself. "I will not be myself again until Banquo's spirit is laid to rest. Only the witches can set me free!"

The witches were
seated in a huddle
around a fire, over
which a cauldron
bubbled. In the sky
above their heads
a full moon sailed,
casting silver light
over the battlefield, still littered
with unburied corpses.

The blind witch held
up her crystal. Deep
inside, a tiny horse
and rider galloped
wildly through
the night. "He
comes!" she
cackled. "The spell
is still strong!"

And Macbeth came out of the moonlight, his horse's flanks white with lathered sweat. He climbed from the saddle and was about to speak when the hook-nosed witch called out, "The King wishes to know the future!"

"It is not for the faint-hearted!" warned the bearded witch.

"I have courage enough!" Macbeth growled.

The blind witch dipped a wooden cup into the cauldron, and held it out. "Drink!" she said.

Macbeth took the cup and lifted it to his lips, shuddering as he swallowed.

Fire, and ice, and the light of the moon burned in his brain.

The blind witch's face melted like the edge of a cloud, and became the face of Duncan, his silver hair dark with blood. "Beware Macduff, the Thane of Fife!" Duncan said, and then he changed into Banquo. "No man born of a woman can harm you," Banquo said. "You will rule until Birnam Wood walks to Dunsinane."

"Then I am safe!" cried Macbeth. "No one can stop me!"

And he was alone: the witches, their cauldron and the fire had vanished.

\* \* \*

It was the start of a fearful time. On his return to Dunsinane, Macbeth ordered that Macduff be arrested. When he heard that Macduff had fled to England to join Malcolm, Macbeth had Macduff's castle burned, and his wife and children put to death. From then on, anyone who questioned the King's commands – no matter how harsh or unjust those commands might be – was executed.

The gap between Macbeth and his wife grew wider. The guilty secret of Duncan's murder gnawed at Lady Macbeth's mind like a maggot inside an apple. She fell ill and began to walk in her sleep, dreaming that she and Macbeth were still covered with Duncan's blood. "Out, damned stain!" she croaked. "Will nothing make me clean?" Doctors could do nothing for her, and she grew weaker every day.

\* \* \*

Then at last hope came to Macbeth's suffering subjects. Malcolm had raised an army in England and, with Macduff at his side, he marched his troops into Scotland. There the army was greeted by cheering crowds, who longed to be freed from the tyrant Macbeth.

First Glamis Castle was captured and
burned, and then Malcolm's forces
marched on to Dunsinane. To the despair
of Macbeth's generals, he did nothing.

Each time they advised him to go to
battle, he laughed and said, "I have
nothing to fear until the day that Birnam
Wood walks to Dunsinane."

✳ ✳ ✳

Through the windows of the throne room, Macbeth could see the distant campfires of Malcolm's army. He raised a cup of wine to them. "Fools!" he jeered. "You cannot overthrow me!"

A sound made him turn. A servant was standing at the door, wringing his hands and weeping.

"What is it?" Macbeth asked gruffly.

"The Queen, my lord," said the servant. "She is...dead."

For a long time, Macbeth was silent, remembering the early years of his marriage, when the world had seemed bright. "Life goes on, day after day, but it means nothing," he said in a cracked whisper. "It ends in despair, and darkness... and death."

Macbeth did not sleep that night. He drank cup after cup of wine, but it brought him no comfort. Only the certainty that his enemies would be defeated and that he would remain unharmed, gave him any hope.

At dawn, an anxious-faced captain brought the King strange news. "The enemy is approaching, my lord," he said. "To conceal the strength of their numbers, they are hiding behind branches cut from Birnam Wood. It looks as though a forest is on the march."

"My curse upon you, witches!" howled Macbeth. "You deceived me! I have lost everything, but at least I can die like a soldier, with a sword in my hand! Go tell the servants to bring my armour!"

It was a short battle. Macbeth's army had no stomach for a fight to protect a king they now hated, and the soldiers began to surrender to Malcolm's men – first in a trickle, then in a flood.

Macbeth fought recklessly, as though he wished to be killed, but he hacked down opponent after opponent, shouting, "You were born of woman!" as he delivered the death blow.

At last, Macbeth found himself alone. He was resting against a cart, when he heard someone call his name. It was Macduff, striding through the smoke of battle, his broadsword at the ready. "I have come to avenge my wife and children!" Macduff said through clenched teeth.

"Stay back!" warned Macbeth. "I cannot be harmed by a man born of woman."

"My mother died before I was born," said Macduff, his eyes blazing with hate. "To save me, the doctor cut me from her body."

Macbeth threw back his head and laughed bitterly. He saw now that all the witches' promises had been lies, and that by believing them, he had betrayed himself. The force that had dominated him was gone, and only his courage remained. "Come then, Macduff!" he cried. "Make an end of me!"

Macduff struck off Macbeth's head with a single sweep of his sword.

The head was placed on top of a spear
that had been driven into the ground
outside the gates of Dunsinane. The
victorious army cheered, then marched
away to see Malcolm crowned King.

As the sun set, three ravens flapped down
from the castle walls and fluttered around
Macbeth's head. "All hail, Macbeth!" they
cawed. "All hail! All hail!"

*Out, out, brief candle.*
*Life's but a walking shadow, a poor player*
*That struts and frets his hour upon the stage,*
*And then is heard no more.*

Macbeth; V.v.

# Evil in Macbeth

Shakespeare wrote *Macbeth* in 1605, four years after James I came to the throne. King James had written a book about witchcraft, and Shakespeare wove three witches into *Macbeth,* to flatter the new monarch, who had granted Shakespeare's acting company the title of *The King's Men* in 1603.

Shakespeare's witches do not simply cast wicked spells. Their prophecies and promises play on Macbeth's mind, bringing out a long-kept secret – his ambition to be king.

The evil in the play does not come from the witches, but from Macbeth himself. Urged on by his wife, Macbeth murders the saintly King Duncan, condemns the king's sons as murderers, and is proclaimed king by the Scots noblemen.

Macbeth's dark dream has come true, but his life turns into a nightmare. To keep the throne he has his best friend murdered, and puts to death anyone who dares oppose him. The brave general has become a cruel tyrant.

In the end, Macbeth loses everything. His wife goes mad and dies, and when an English army invades Scotland his noblemen turn against him. The promises the witches made to Macbeth prove to be hollow, and he dies at the hands of Macduff, whose wife and children he had executed.

With its three witches, a ghost and a phantom dagger, *Macbeth* was the sixteenth-century equivalent of a modern horror movie. But the real horror lies in the change that comes over Macbeth's character. The potential for evil, Shakespeare seems to suggest, is lurking inside us all, and we must constantly be on guard against it.

# Twelfth Night

# Cast List

## Sebastian and Viola

Twin brother and sister

## Olivia

A rich Countess

## Orsino

Duke of Illyria

## Malvolio

Steward to Olivia

## Sir Toby Belch

Uncle to Olivia

## Sir Andrew Aguecheek

Friend to Sir Toby

## A Sailor

# The Scene

Coastal Illyria, fifteenth century.

*If music be the food of love, play on,*
*Give me excess of it,*

Orsino; I.i.

# Twelfth Night

Sebastian and his twin sister Viola were as alike as two raindrops. They had the same light brown hair, bright blue eyes and winning smiles. Sometimes, when they were children, Viola used to borrow Sebastian's clothes and pretend to be him – which confused everybody.

The twins grew up together, were taught together, and they almost died together. That was on the day the ship in which they were travelling foundered on a treacherous

reef and sank. Viola saved herself by
clinging to Sebastian's clothes-trunk, and
was washed up on the coast of Illyria.

As she was a practical, quick-thinking person, Viola decided she would be safer if she disguised herself as a young man, so she tied up her hair, dressed in clothes that she took from her brother's trunk and called herself Cesario. She prayed that Sebastian had survived the shipwreck and for three days she sought news of him, but then her money ran out, so, still disguised as Cesario, she found a job as a page to Duke Orsino, ruler of Illyria.

Orsino was delighted with his new page, and before long, Viola had won his confidence, and he had won her heart. The Duke was tall, dark, handsome, rich, and popular with his people – and yet he was not content. He moped about his palace during the day, and in the evening listened to troubadours singing sad songs. He never laughed, and hardly ever smiled.

Like many young
women before her,
Viola found herself
falling in love with
Orsino and it was
painful to keep her
feelings a secret. The
pain became even worse
when, one day when they were alone

together, she summoned
up the courage to
ask why he was
so unhappy.
"Because
I am suffering
from the worst
sickness in the
world – love!"
Orsino replied.

"I'm so in love with Countess Olivia that I don't know what to do, Cesario! I've asked her to marry me a dozen times, but she keeps refusing."

"She must be mad!" said Viola. "If you asked me to – I mean, if I were a woman, I would marry you at once, my lord!"

Orsino sighed, then suddenly he had an idea that seemed so brilliant, that for a moment he looked almost happy. "You know, Cesario, I think you could gain Olivia's trust as quickly as you have gained mine," he said thoughtfully. "Go and see her today. Tell her that if she won't marry me, I'll waste away and die!"

"Me, my lord?" gulped Viola.

Orsino placed his hand on Viola's shoulder. "You're my last hope!"

'So I must try and persuade Countess Olivia to marry the man I love!' Viola thought ruefully. 'Why does life have to be so complicated?'

Though she did not realise it at that moment, Viola's life was about to become more complicated than she could possibly imagine.

Countess Olivia's
parents had died
when she was
still young and
her uncle, Sir
Toby Belch, had
come to live with her.
Sir Toby was short and
plump, with white whiskers and twinkling
blue eyes, and his love of wine and good

food had turned his nose
bright red. His
closest friend
was Sir Andrew
Aguecheek, a
man with a
face as long
and wrinkled as
a bloodhound's.

Since Sir Andrew was a bachelor, Sir Toby had decided that he would make the perfect husband for his niece, Olivia. However, Olivia's steward, Malvolio, protected her from all unwanted suitors, including Sir Andrew!

On the day that Orsino sent Viola
to plead with Olivia, Sir Toby and Sir
Andrew were plotting together in the
library of Olivia's house.

"If I could only be alone with her for
five minutes!" Sir Andrew grumbled. "But
Malvolio will not let me see her. He won't
even give her my letters."

"My niece has given him far too much control of her affairs, and it's gone to his head," grumbled Sir Tony. "Why, the other evening, the scoundrel actually had the impudence to tell me that I drink too much!"

"The villain!" said Sir Andrew.

"But I intend to teach him a lesson," Sir Toby said, with a mischievous grin. "Mark my words, old friend, before the day is over, Malvolio will be out of your way."

✳ ✳ ✳

While her uncle schemed in the library, Olivia was strolling in the garden with Malvolio at her side. With his skinny body and black clothes, Malvolio resembled a bony shadow. "A young man called Cesario wishes to see you, my lady," he was saying to her. "He brings a message from the Duke Orsino."

"Tell him to go away!" said Olivia, and her green eyes flashed as she tossed her dark-red hair in irritation.

"I have, my lady," said Malvolio. "But he says he will stand at the gate all afternoon if he has to." Malvolio sniffed haughtily. "He is a most insolent young fellow!"

"Oh, let me see him, then!" Olivia said wearily. "Perhaps, when he hears my reply, Orsino will finally abandon all hope of marrying me!"

When Viola entered the garden, Olivia pretended to be interested in the blossoms on a rose bush, and gave Orsino's new messenger no more than a glance.

"Sweet lady," said Viola. "Now I see how beautiful you are, I understand why my master is so in love with you!" Olivia, who hated flattery of any kind, snorted scornfully. "Beautiful?" she said. "I have two eyes, a nose and a mouth like everybody else, if that's what you mean!"

"Ah, so you are proud as well as lovely!" said Viola. "It is a pity that the Duke loves a lady with such a hard heart."

"Orsino doesn't really love me!" Olivia declared. "He's just in love with the idea of being in love. Go and tell him I cannot make myself love him just because he wants me to!" She looked up from the roses, and as she did so, she saw quite the most beautiful young man she had ever met.

Her head swam giddily and her heart began to pound. "Tell Orsino that I will never marry him," she said breathlessly.

"And then...
come back
to see me at
once, Cesario."

"Why?"
frowned Viola.

"Er...to tell me
how he responds
to my answer!"
Olivia said with a blush.

Viola bowed and turned to go, leaving
Olivia alone with a whirlwind of thoughts
and feelings she had never experienced
before. One moment, Olivia wanted to
laugh out loud, and the next, she wanted
to burst into tears. She was so confused,
that she did not notice Malvolio
approaching. He seemed to drop out of
the sky and land in front of her.

"I hope that young man did not offend you, my lady?" Malvolio said.

"Offend me?" said Olivia. "Why, no. I mean – yes, yes he did!" On impulse, she pulled a ring from one of her fingers. "He brought me this gift from the Duke. Return the ring to Cesario and tell him I don't want it!"

"Of course, my lady," Malvolio said smoothly. "Where is the fellow?"

"Gone," said Olivia. "If you run, you'll soon catch up with him."

"What, run – I?" gasped Malvolio; then he bowed politely as he saw the angry green fire in Olivia's eyes. "I'll go at once!" he said.

\* \* \*

Viola walked slowly. Her heart was heavy for Orsino, and herself, and when a voice from behind called out, "Cesario?" for a moment she forgot that it was the name she had given herself, and did not remember until the voice called out again. "Cesario! Ho, there!"

Viola turned and saw Malvolio running towards her, his elbows sticking out and his knobbly knees pumping up and down. This was surprise enough, but Viola was completely astonished when Malvolio offered her a ring. "You brought my lady this!" he panted. "Now she wants you to take it back."

"I didn't give her a ring!" said Viola.
Malvolio peevishly stamped his foot
and threw the ring to the ground. "Let it
lie there, then!" he snapped. "I have
better things to do than argue with the
likes of you!" He turned on his heel and
marched angrily away.

Viola stooped
and picking up
the ring, saw
on it a design
of two hands
holding a heart.
'But this is a love
token!' she thought.
'Young women don't send love tokens to
other young women!' The
truth fell on her like
an avalanche.
"Oh, no!" she
cried. "Olivia
thinks I'm a
man – and
she's fallen in
love with me!"

Orsino was alone when Viola found him. He was singing a song about doomed lovers and how, no matter how brightly the sun shone, somewhere the rain was sure to be pouring down like tears.

Viola waited until the song was over, then told Orsino what Olivia had said.

Orsino closed his eyes. "Ah!" he groaned tragically. "If you knew what agony love can be, Cesario!"

"Oh, I do, my lord!" Viola said.

Orsino unpinned a brooch from his doublet and handed it to Viola. "Then go to Olivia again," he said. "Give her this brooch and tell her that even though she will not be my wife, my love will last as long as the diamonds that are set into it!"

Meanwhile Malvolio had returned to the garden. Olivia was not there, but as he hurried towards the house to find her, he found a letter lying on the path and picked it up.

"Why, this is my lady's handwriting!"
Malvolio murmured. "Since I am her
steward, and her business is my business,
it is my duty to read it!" He was so
interested in the letter that he failed to
see Sir Toby and Sir Andrew, hidden in a
bank of laurel bushes nearby.

"To M, *my dearest love*," Malvolio read aloud. "*Though you are my servant, you are master of my heart. Be bold, and my hand is yours! If you love me, wear yellow tights, cross-gartered, as a secret sign.*" Malvolio clutched the letter to his bosom. "Olivia loves me!" he burbled. "I must change into yellow tights at once!"

As soon as Malvolio was out of sight, the laurel bushes began to shake with laughter. "I knew it would work!" Sir Toby told Sir Andrew. "I can imitate my niece's handwriting well enough to deceive anybody! Now all we have to do is…"

"Hush!" said Sir Andrew. "Someone is coming!"

\* \* \*

Olivia and Viola were deep in conversation. They stopped in front of a bank of laurel bushes, and Viola said, "Then you have no new answer for the Duke?"

"No!" said Olivia, clutching Viola's hand. "But there are answers I would give to you, Cesario, if you would only ask me the questions!"

Viola gently took her hand away. "My lady, I am not all that I seem to be," she said tactfully.

"But I love you!" exclaimed Olivia. "I loved you from the first moment I set eyes on you."

"You might as well love a dream," Viola said. "You must forget me, my lady!" and she slipped away, leaving Olivia in tears.

In the bushes, Sir Andrew quivered with rage. "That chit of a youth has stolen Olivia's love!" he hissed.

"After him!" urged Sir Toby. "Challenge him to a duel! That should see him off!"

"A duel?" said Sir Andrew, alarmed.

"He won't dare to fight you!" said Sir Toby. "That Cesario is nothing but a puny milksop – he'll turn tail and run the moment you draw your sword!"

While Sir Andrew went to waylay Viola at the garden gate, Olivia stumbled towards the house, her eyes filled with tears. "Oh, Cesario!" she whispered. "I must see you again, if only for a second!"

Then she saw Malvolio walking towards her. He was wearing yellow tights as bright as canaries, and his face was stretched into a ghastly smile. "Well met, my angel!" he simpered.

"Malvolio?" said Olivia. "Are you feeling quite well?"

"Never better, my sweetness!" Malvolio purred, stretching out his leg. "Have you noticed my yellow tights and cross-garters?"

"I could hardly miss them!" Olivia replied. "I think the heat has made you feverish. Wouldn't you like to lie down?"

"Yes, with you by my side!" said
Malvolio.

"Help!" cried Olivia. "Servants, take
Malvolio away! He has lost his wits!"

✳ ✳ ✳

Meanwhile, Viola, relieved to be going back to her master, the Duke, suddenly found herself face to face with a furious Sir Andrew Aguecheek.

"Draw your sword, vile scoundrel!" snarled Sir Andrew.

"My sword?" Viola quailed. "But why?"

"So I can fight you!" Sir Andrew said. "Or are you a coward as well as a villain?"

Reluctantly, Viola reached for her sword with a trembling hand, and at that same moment, most fortunately a loud voice shouted, "Stop!"

A hefty sailor appeared through the gateway.

"If you harm one hair of this young man's head," he warned Sir Andrew, "I'll carve you up like a joint of beef!"

"Oh!" said Sir Andrew, pale with fear.
"Oh, well in that case, I think I'd
better..." and he ran away at an
impressive speed.

Viola felt weak with relief. "How can
I ever thank you, kind stranger?" she
said to the sailor.

"Stranger?" scowled the sailor. "That's a fine thing to call the man who saved you from drowning and helped you to try and find your lost sister! I've been waiting for you at the inn down the road for the last two days, Sebastian!"

"*Sebastian?*" gasped Viola. "Then my brother is alive and well!"

✳ ✳ ✳

Sebastian was alive and well, but totally
bewildered. On his way to meet the sailor
who had saved him, he happened to pass
a fine house out of which rushed
a beautiful red-haired
young woman. "I
knew you would
come back, Cesario!"
she said, flinging
her arms around
him. "We cannot
live without
each other!"

"But, my lady,"
Sebastian said.

"Call me Olivia,
my dearest!"
said Olivia.

Sebastian looked into Olivia's eyes. He was about to tell her that she had made a terrible mistake, and that his name was not Cesario, but

then his heart began to beat faster as love worked its magic on him. "This must be a dream!" he said softly. "But please, don't wake me up yet!" And he hugged Olivia tightly.

The two of them were still embracing when Viola and the sailor discovered them. Sebastian recognised his sister and ran to her with a joyous shout. He lifted Viola high into the air, while Olivia and the sailor looked on open-mouthed.

"Are there two of him?" whispered
Olivia. "I don't understand."

"It seems so," said the sailor, scratching
his head. "If you ask me, my lady,
someone has a lot of explaining to do!"

\* \* \*

Duke Orsino waited two anxious hours for Cesario to return, and at last he lost his patience. He called for his fastest horse, and galloped to Olivia's house.

In the hall, he was met with the strangest sight – Cesario and Olivia, arm in arm, and behind them, a smiling priest holding a bible.

"Cesario!" Orsino thundered. "Release that lady!"

"This is not Cesario, my lord," Olivia beamed. "This is Sebastian, who will soon be my husband. If you seek the one you called Cesario, look behind you!"

Orsino turned
and saw Viola,
wearing a dress
that Olivia had
lent her. She
looked so lovely
that she quite took

Orsino's breath away, and he instantly
fell head over heels in love with her.

"If you take my advice, you'll marry her
straightaway," Olivia
told the Duke. "She
loves you with
all her heart!"
"And now I
see her as her
rightful self, I love
her with all mine!"
Orsino declared.

And so there was a double wedding in the house of Countess Olivia, and that night the windows were bright with lights, and the air was filled with the sounds of music and celebration.

The laughter and singing rang through the house, and reached the ears of Malvolio, who had been locked in the cellar. He pressed his face against the bars of the window and called out, "Hello, hello! Let me out, someone! I am not mad – truly I am not!"

But nobody heard him, not that night.

*I'll follow this good man, and go with you,*
*And having sworn truth, ever will be true.*

Sebastian; V.i.

# Appearance in Twelfth Night

It's easy for people to get identical twins mixed up. In *Twelfth Night*, Shakespeare uses this idea with hilarious results.

Beneath the comedy, though, Shakespeare makes a serious point about how we judge people by the way they look. Viola dresses as a man, and everyone assumes that she is one. Malvolio is tricked into wearing bright yellow tights, and makes himself look ridiculous.

When Viola dresses in her brother Sebastian's clothes and pretends to be Cesario, she has no idea of what it will lead to. She falls in love with Duke Orsino, but can't tell him because he thinks that she is a man. Then Countess Olivia falls in love with Cesario, and things become *really* complicated.

Part of the fun for an Elizabethan audience came from the fact that all the female parts were played by boys. So when Viola appears as Cesario, the actor would have been a boy pretending to be a girl pretending to be a boy – as if the story weren't complicated enough!

As in most of his comedies, Shakespeare pokes fun at people in love. Orsino believes he loves Olivia, but actually he is in love with being in love. When Olivia falls for Cesario, she is transformed from a sensible, independent young woman to a lovesick teenager.

Shakespeare shows how misleading appearances can be, and that what is in peoples' hearts is far more important than the clothes they wear.

# Romeo and Juliet

# Cast List

## Juliet
Daughter of Lord Capulet

## Romeo
Son of Lord Montague

## Mercutio
Friend to Romeo

## Benvolio
Friend and cousin to Romeo

## Tybalt
Cousin to Juliet

Nurse to Juliet

Friar Lawrence

Lord Capulet

The Prince of Verona

A Monk
Messenger to
Friar Lawrence

# The Scene

Verona in the fifteenth century.

*But soft, what light through yonder*
*window breaks?*
*It is the east, and Juliet is the sun.*

Romeo; II.i.

# Romeo and Juliet

On that warm summer's evening, the Capulet house was the brightest place in Verona. The walls of the ballroom were hung with silk tapestries, and candle-light from a dozen crystal chandeliers threw rainbows on to the heads of the masked dancers as they twirled through the music and laughter that filled the air.

On one side of the room, near a table laden with food and drink, stood a young girl, Juliet, the daughter of Lord and Lady Capulet. She had removed her mask and loosened her black hair so that it hung about her shoulders. Her face, flushed from the heat of the dance, was radiant

and her beauty was obvious to all who looked at her. She seemed unaware that someone was watching her.

A few steps away, a young man stood gazing at her. He had never seen such loveliness before in his whole life.

'Surely I must be mistaken!' he thought. 'Surely, if I look a second time, I will find that her eyes are too close together, her nose too long or her mouth too wide!' Moving slowly towards her, as one in a trance, the young man lifted his mask so that he could see Juliet more clearly – and the more he gazed at her, the more perfect her face seemed.

Almost without thinking, Romeo
pushed his way towards Juliet until he
found himself standing at her side. Gently
he took her hand.

Juliet turned her head, her soft brown
eyes wide with surprise.

✳ ✳ ✳

On the other side of the room, Tybalt, Lord Capulet's fiery young nephew, recognised the young man who was holding Juliet's hand, and strode angrily towards the door; but just as he was about to leave, his uncle caught him by the sleeve.

"Where are you going?" asked Lord Capulet.

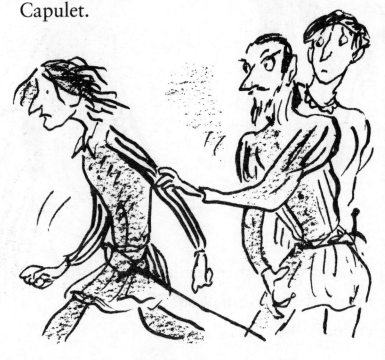

"To fetch my rapier," Tybalt replied. "Lord Montague's son, Romeo, has dared to enter the house!"

"Leave him!" said Lord Capulet.

There was a terrible feud between the Capulets and the Montagues and the Prince of Verona had forbidden any more fighting between the two families, on pain of death.

Tybalt's face was ashen with rage. "But tomorrow, Romeo will boast to his friends about how he danced at the Capulets' ball and escaped without being noticed! He will make us look like fools!"

Lord Capulet put his hands on Tybalt's shoulders, forcing him to stop and listen.

"I hate the Montagues as deeply as you do, Tybalt," he said. "Our two families have been at war with each other for as long as anyone can remember – but the Prince's word is law in this city, and there is to be no more fighting – you understand? Now, if you cannot keep your temper like a man, go to your room and sulk like a boy!"

Tybalt broke free from his uncle's grasp
and glared across the room at Romeo.
"You will pay for this one day, Montague!"
he vowed softly. "I will make you pay!"

\* \* \*

Juliet glanced at the young man beside her, at his glossy brown hair and startlingly grey eyes that were filled with shyness and wonder. His mouth was curved in a half-smile, and though it made her blush to look, Juliet found that she could not take her eyes from his face, or her hand from his.

"My lady," Romeo said, "if my hand has offended yours by holding it, please forgive me."

"My hand is not offended, sir," said Juliet, smiling at him, "and nor am I."

Some power that neither of them understood had drawn them together like a moth to a flame. They kissed and the ballroom, the musicians and dancers seemed to disappear, leaving them feeling as though they were the only two people in the world.

When their lips parted, Romeo looked at Juliet and thought, 'All those other times, when I thought I was in love, I was like a child playing a game. This time I am truly in love – I wonder, could she possibly feel the same?'

Before he could ask, an elderly woman bustled up to them. "My lady," she said to Juliet, "your mother is asking for you."

Juliet frowned, shrugged helplessly at Romeo, then turned and walked away.

Romeo caught the old woman by the arm. "Do you know that lady?" he demanded.

"Why, sir, she is Juliet, Lord Capulet's daughter," said the woman. "I've been her nurse since she was a baby. And I know who you are, too, young man. Take my advice and leave this house, before there's trouble!"

\* \* \*

That night Juliet couldn't get to sleep. She
could only think of Romeo. It was warm
and the moonlight was shining on the
trees in the orchard below. Juliet stepped
out onto her balcony, but she was so
troubled by what her nurse had told her,
that she hardly noticed how lovely the
orchard looked.

"How can I be in love with someone I ought to hate?" she sighed. "Oh, Romeo, why did you have to be a Montague? If you had been born with any other name, I could tell you how much I love you!"

Romeo stepped out of the shadows of the trees into the moonlight. "Call me your love," he said. "It is the only name I want!"

Juliet looked down from her balcony and gasped. "How did you get here? If anyone catches you, they will kill you!"

"I climbed the orchard wall," said Romeo. "I had to see you again! I loved you the moment I first saw you, and I wanted to know if you felt the same."

Juliet's face brightened with joy, then darkened into doubt. "How can I be sure of your love?" she said. "How can I be sure that you will not forget me as soon as tonight is over?" Romeo looked up into Juliet's eyes and saw the way the moonlight shone in them. He knew he would never love anyone else.

"Meet me at Friar Lawrence's chapel at noon tomorrow, and we shall be married!" Romeo declared.

"Married?" laughed Juliet. "But we have only just met! And what will our parents say?"

"Do we need to meet more than once to know that our love is strong, and real?" said Romeo. "Must we live apart because of our families' hatred?"

A part of Juliet knew that for them to marry would be mad and impossible, but another part of her knew that if she sent Romeo away now, she might never see him again, and she wasn't sure she could bear that. "Yes!" she said.

"Yes, I believe what we feel for each other is true! And yes, I'll meet you tomorrow at the chapel at noon!"

So, the next day Romeo and Juliet were married.

\* \* \*

The bell in the clock tower of the cathedral tolled twice. The main square of Verona sweltered in the hot sunshine and the air shimmered. Two young men were lounging beside a fountain and the taller of the two, Romeo's closest friend, Mercutio, dipped a handkerchief into the water and mopped his face. "Where is he?" he demanded tetchily. "He should have been here an hour ago!"

His companion, Romeo's cousin, Benvolio, smiled at Mercutio's impatience. "Some important business must have detained him," he said.

"A pair of pretty eyes, more like!" snorted Mercutio. But as he glanced across the square, he saw Romeo hurrying towards them. "At last!" Mercutio said sarcastically. "I was beginning to think that the Queen of the Fairies had carried you off in your sleep!"

"I have great news!" said Romeo. "But you must promise to keep it a secret!"

Mercutio looked curiously at his friend. "Oh?" he said.

"I am in love," said Romeo.

Benvolio laughed; Mercutio groaned and shook his head. "You are always in love!" he cried. "A girl only has to look at you sideways to make you fall for her."

"It's more than that this time," said Romeo. "I am in love with…"

"Romeo!" interrupted a harsh voice.

Romeo turned, and saw Tybalt with a group of sneering Capulets. Tybalt's right hand was resting on the hilt of his sword. "You were at my family's house last night," he said. "Now you must pay for your insolence. Draw your sword!"

Romeo's eyes flashed with anger, then grew calm. "I will not fight you, Tybalt," he said. "It would be like fighting one of my own family."

"Why, you milksop!" jeered Tybalt. "You're as cowardly as the rest of the Montagues."

"Romeo!" gasped Mercutio. "Are you going to stand and do nothing while he insults your family?"

"I must," said Romeo. "You don't understand. I have no choice…"

"But I do!" snarled Mercutio.

His rapier flashed in the sunlight as he drew it. "If you want a fight, Tybalt, I'm your man!" he cried.

In a movement too fast to follow, Tybalt brought out his sword and the two young men began to fight at a dazzling speed.

"Help me to stop them, Benvolio!" pleaded Romeo. He caught Mercutio from behind, pinning his arms to his sides. As he did so, Tybalt lunged forward and drove the point of his rapier through Mercutio's heart, fatally wounding him.

"A plague on both your houses," he whispered with his dying breath.

When Romeo realised that his friend was dead, rage surged through him and his hatred of the Capulets brought a bitter taste to his mouth. "Tybalt!" he cried, drawing his rapier. "One of us must join Mercutio in death!"

"Then let our swords decide who it shall be!" Tybalt snarled.

Romeo hacked at Tybalt as though Tybalt were a tree that he wanted to cut down. At first, the watching Capulets laughed at Romeo's clumsiness, but as Tybalt began to fall back towards the centre of the square, their laughter died. It was obvious that Tybalt was tiring and finding it difficult to defend himself.

At last, Romeo and Tybalt stood face to face, their swords locked together. Tybalt's left hand fumbled at his belt and he drew out a dagger. Romeo, seeing the danger, clamped his left hand around Tybalt's wrist, and they stumbled and struggled with each other.

Tybalt flicked out a foot, intending to trip Romeo, but instead he lost his own balance and the two enemies tumbled to the ground. Romeo fell on Tybalt's left hand, forcing the point of the dagger deep into Tybalt's chest. He felt Tybalt's dying breath warm against his cheek.

A voice called out, "Quick! The Prince's guards!" and the Capulets scattered.

Benvolio helped Romeo to his feet.
"Come now, before it is too late," he said,
but Romeo did not hear him. He stared at
Tybalt's body, and the full realisation of
what he had done fell on him like a weight.

'I have killed Juliet's cousin!' he thought. 'She cannot love a murderer! She will never forgive me! How could I have let myself be such a fool!'

He was still staring at Tybalt when the Prince's guards reached him.

✳ ✳ ✳

That night, the Prince of Verona passed judgement on Romeo. "The hatred of the Montagues and Capulets has cost two lives today," he said. "I want no more bloodshed. I will spare Romeo his life, but I banish him to the city of Mantua. He must leave tonight, and if he is ever found in Verona again, he will be put to death!"

\* \* \*

When Friar Lawrence heard the news of Romeo's banishment, he was deeply upset. He had already married Romeo and Juliet in secret, hoping that one day, their love would overcome the hatred between the Montagues and the Capulets – but it seemed that the hate had been too strong. After his evening meal, the Friar went to his chapel to say a prayer for the young lovers.

As he knelt in front of the altar, Friar Lawrence heard the sound of the chapel door opening, and footsteps racing up the aisle. He stood, turned and saw Juliet, who flung herself sobbing at his feet.

"Help me, Friar Lawrence!" she begged. "My father wants me to marry Count Paris, but I'd rather die than forsake Romeo."

"Do not despair, my child," Friar Lawrence urged. "Surely you can reason with your father?"

"I could not bring myself to tell him about Romeo," Juliet sobbed. "I pleaded Tybalt's death had made me too full of grief to think of marriage. But Father would not listen and the wedding is to take place tomorrow."

Friar Lawrence looked troubled. "There may be a way for you and Romeo to be together, my child, but it is dangerous," he said.

Friar Lawrence took a tiny bottle of blue liquid from the pouch at his belt. "Drink this tonight," he said, "and you will fall into a sleep as deep as death. Your parents will believe that you are dead and will put your body into the Capulet tomb – but in two days you will wake, alive and well."

"And Romeo?" said Juliet.

"I will send him a message explaining everything," said Friar Lawrence. "After you wake, you can go to Mantua in secret."

And so, on the morning of Juliet's wedding to Paris, the screams of her nurse woke the whole Capulet house.

When the news of Juliet's death reached Benvolio, he rode straight to Mantua to Romeo. One of the travellers he passed on the way was a monk, who recognised him. "Lord Benvolio!" he called out as Benvolio approached.

"I have a letter for your cousin Romeo from Friar Lawrence!"

"Out of my way!" Benvolio shouted back. "I have no time to stop!"

The monk watched as Benvolio galloped by on the road to Mantua. At that speed, the monk judged, Benvolio would be in the city before evening.

✳ ✳ ✳

When Benvolio told Romeo that Juliet
was dead, Romeo's heart broke and for
hours he lay sobbing on his bed, while
outside day turned into night. During that
time, Benvolio stayed at Romeo's side,
but he had no idea how to comfort his
grief-stricken friend.

It was almost
midnight before
Romeo grew calm
enough to speak.
He sat up and
wiped away his
tears with the
back of his
hand. "I must go
to her," he said.

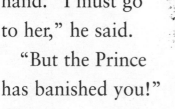

"But the Prince
has banished you!"
Benvolio reminded him. "If you are seen
on the streets of Verona, it will mean
your death."

"I am not afraid of death," said Romeo.
"Without Juliet, my life means nothing.
Go wake the grooms, and tell them to
saddle my horse."

When Benvolio had left him alone, Romeo searched through the wooden chest at the foot of his bed until he found 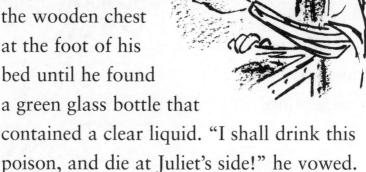 a green glass bottle that contained a clear liquid. "I shall drink this poison, and die at Juliet's side!" he vowed.

Romeo left Mantua at daybreak, refusing to let Benvolio accompany him.

Once out of the city, he travelled along winding country tracks so that he could approach Verona without being seen.

It was night when he arrived and with the hood of his cloak drawn up to hide his face, he slipped in unrecognised through the city walls at the main gate.

He went straight to the Capulet tomb, and it was almost as if someone had expected him, for the door was unlocked, and the interior was lit by a burning torch.

Romeo looked around, saw Tybalt's body, pale as candle wax – then Juliet, laid out on a marble slab, her death-shroud as white as a bridal gown. With a cry, Romeo rushed to her side and covered her

face with kisses and tears. "I cannot live without you," he whispered. "I want your beauty to be the last thing my eyes see. We could not be together in life, my sweet love, but in death, nothing shall part us!"

Romeo drew
the cork from
the poison
bottle and
raised it to his
lips. He felt the
vile liquid sting
his throat. Then
darkness swallowed him.

For a time, there was no sound except
the spluttering of the torch;
then Juliet began
to breathe. She
moaned, opened
her eyes, and saw
Romeo dead at
her side with the
empty poison
bottle in his hand.

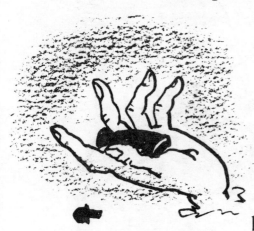

At first, she thought she was dreaming, but when she reached out to touch Romeo's face, and smelled the bitter scent of the poison, she knew that the nightmare was real, and that Friar Lawrence's plan had gone terribly wrong. She cradled Romeo in her arms and rocked him, weeping into his hair.

"If you had only waited a little longer!" Juliet whispered, and she kissed Romeo again and again, desperately hoping that there was enough

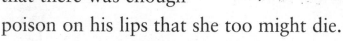

poison on his lips that she too might die.

Then she saw the torchlight gleam on the dagger at Romeo's belt. She drew the weapon and pressed its point to her heart. "Now, dagger, take me to my love!" she said, and pushed with all her strength.

Friar Lawrence found the lovers a few hours later. They were huddled together like sleeping children.

\* \* \*

When Romeo and Juliet died, the hatred between the Montagues and Capulets died with them. United by grief, the two families agreed that Romeo and Juliet should be buried together. They paid for a statue of the lovers to be set over the grave, and on the base of the statue these words were carved:

> *There never was a story of more woe*
> *Than this of Juliet and Romeo.*

*The sun for sorrow will not show his head.*
*Go hence, to have more talk of these sad things.*

The Prince of Verona; V.iii.

# Love and Hate in Romeo and Juliet

In *Romeo and Juliet*, Shakespeare weaves together two of the most powerful human emotions, love and hate.

The bitter hatred in *Romeo and Juliet* results from the feud between the Montagues and Capulets, two rich families in the Italian city of Verona. The feud has led to so many gang-fights in the streets that the Prince of Verona has ordered the fighting to stop, on pain of death.

The passionate love comes from Romeo and Juliet, who fall in love at first sight at a ball in the Capulets' house. Juliet is a Capulet, Romeo is a Montague, and the moment their lips meet, their fate is sealed. Tybalt, Juliet's cousin, sees them together and swears to take revenge for what he considers an insult to his family.

Shakespeare shows us how strangely alike love and hate are in the way they make people act without thinking. Hate causes the death of both Mercutio, Romeo's best friend, and Tybalt, Juliet's cousin. Love leads Romeo and Juliet into a chain of tragic events. Their happy wedding sets them on the road to a sorry end.

At the end of the play, the young lovers are dead, and the Montagues and Capulets are brought together at last, united by another powerful emotion – grief. The love and the hate have cancelled each other out, and all that is left is sadness.

# Antony and Cleopatra

# Cast List

### Servius
Storyteller
Bodyguard to Antony

### Cleopatra
Queen of Egypt

### Mark Antony
One of the three rulers of Rome

# Octavius Caesar and Lepidus

Rulers of Rome with Antony

# Antony's Generals

# The Scene

Ancient Egypt and Rome.

*Eternity was in our lips and eyes,*
*Bliss in our brow's bent; none our parts so poor*
*But was a race of heaven.*

Cleopatra; I.iii.

# Antony and Cleopatra

You want to know about Antony and Cleopatra? Let me tell you the story – the real story.

I was there at the start, the night Julius Caesar was killed and Antony made a speech over his body in the Market Place.

As soon as Antony stood before us, pale and proud in the torchlight, my heart went out to him. He spoke in a voice like the beating of a war drum, and by the time he had finished speaking, I knew I would follow him anywhere – to the shores of Hades and beyond, if he asked me to.

When civil war broke out, I was one of the first to join Antony's legions. It was a bitter, bloody struggle: Roman against Roman, each believing that right was on his side. I was commended for my courage in action – though all I did was keep my head and obey orders – and Antony himself promoted me to the rank of centurion, just before the battle of Philippi.

That's where I got this scar on my neck, but I was lucky. Braver men than I died that day, including Brutus, who killed himself to escape the shame of defeat. Antony wept at the sight of Brutus's corpse, and many of us wept with him.

Then came the peace, though few believed that it would last. The Empire was carved like a goose, and divided up between the three victors. War makes for strange alliances, but none as strange as that trio. Octavius Caesar, Julius Caesar's nephew, was as ruthless and cold as Antony was warm and generous; Lepidus, the third ally, was a joke – a jellyfish with no sting. Caesar took the West, Antony the East, and Lepidus the African provinces that were left over.

Almost straight away there was trouble in the East. The Parthians invaded Roman territory, and Antony sailed out with his legions to deal with them. There was a

battle – of sorts. The Parthians were
poorly armed, and undisciplined; most of
them turned and ran the moment they
saw the sunlight shining on our shields.

After the victory, Antony called me to his tent. "Well, Servius," he said, "your centurion days are over."

I thought he was going to pension me off and send me back to Rome. "Why, sir?" I protested.

Antony gave me one of his boyish grins. "Because I want you to join my bodyguard," he said. "I need good fighters about me, men I can trust – and I know I can rely on you."

I was lost for words. My heart beat so proudly that I thought it would burst my armour.

"We leave for Tarsus tonight," Antony said. "I have commanded Queen Cleopatra of Egypt to meet me there, to answer charges that she supplied Brutus with troops and money. I want you at my side. I wouldn't put it past her to slip a hired assassin into the crowds."

"While I've breath in my body, no assassin will get past me to strike at you, sir," I said, and I meant every word.

There was gossip on the road to Tarsus, all of it about Cleopatra, and little of it worth repeating. Men said she was a beauty, who had charmed Julius Caesar and made him fawn over her like a dog. Now, the story went, she planned to do the same with Antony, but I would have none of it. "Caesar was past his prime," I said. "Antony is still young, and his wife is a member of one of Rome's most powerful families. It will take more than some Egyptian woman to make him forget where his loyalty lies, even if she is a queen."

How the Gods must have laughed when they heard that!

A few days later, I was on the quayside at Tarsus with Antony, waiting for Cleopatra's royal barge to arrive. It was more than two hours late, and Antony was annoyed. "This is an insult!" he kept muttering. "That little Nile serpent means to make me look a fool!"

But at last we heard distant voices on the wind: women's voices, singing a twisting, slithering melody that my ears could not follow. Cleopatra's barge rounded a bend in the river, and the watching crowds gasped.

The hull, deck and oars of the barge had

been gilded, so that the boat looked like a
fire burning on the water. The sails were
deep purple and scented and the breeze
that filled them carried the fragrance
across the harbour. I breathed in the
perfume of Egypt for the first time: a spicy,
honeyed smell that made my head swim.

The barge drew close, and I caught my first glimpse of Cleopatra. Her robes were cloth of gold, and she wore the double crown of Egypt. Her skin was golden-brown, her hair black, and glossy as a horse's flank; her huge, dark eyes were deep and still. I had heard tales that Helen of Troy was the most beautiful woman ever, but when I saw Cleopatra, I knew that Helen had been eclipsed.

"This is no Queen!" Antony said softly. "This is a Goddess!"

Cleopatra stepped onto the quay, and the cheering crowds sounded like storm waves breaking.

Antony stepped forward and said, "In the name of the Senate and People of Rome, I greet you, and require you to…" He broke off in astonishment as Cleopatra knelt at his feet and bowed her head.

The crowds fell silent.

Antony frowned, then bent down, and helped Cleopatra to her feet. "My noble lord does me too much honour," she said, her head still lowered.

"There is much to discuss," said Antony, "but this is not a fit place. Dine with me tonight, in the city."

"No, my lord,"
Cleopatra said.

'No' was not
a word that
Antony was used
to hearing, and I saw
him stiffen in anger; but
then Cleopatra looked up at him. "Dine
with me, on the barge," she said. "Let me
see if my Egyptian cooks can please you.

Eat with me and taste new

delights, my lord."

Antony looked

into Cleopatra's

eyes, and his

anger melted.

"Now I am

the honoured

one," he said.

I knew then that he had fallen in love with her, as surely as if I had seen one of Eros's arrows pierce his heart.

Within a week, we set sail for Egypt, and nothing was ever the same again.

\* \* \*

Egypt was another world. Beyond the Nile's green valley stretched the desert, unchanging and timeless. In Egypt, the years slipped away like a handful of water.

Antony grew older and softer. He seemed to care for nothing but Cleopatra and their children. Some of the soldiers became restless, saying that Antony was not the man he had once been, and that Cleopatra had bewitched him. Such talk made me angry. "You'll see Antony's greatness again when the time comes!" I said.

And the time came. There was chaos in Rome: Antony's wife, Fulvia, and Lucius, his brother, raised an army to overthrow Octavius Caesar and were crushed in battle. Fulvia died on her way to see Antony in Egypt.

At the same time, Sextus Pompeius rebelled against Caesar, and the Parthians invaded the Roman territories at their borders.

The world of Rome seemed about to collapse.

I was with Antony when the dispatches reached him. His face darkened as he read them, and for a long time he brooded in silence. "Is it true, Servius?" he asked at last. "Am I really as old and weak as they say?"

"You are Mark Antony, sir," I told him.

Something of his old look shone in Antony's eyes. "I will go to Rome and settle my differences with Caesar," he said. "If he, I and Lepidus make peace with Pompeius, we can put our forces together, defeat the Parthians and save Rome before it is too late." Then his face fell. "But what shall I tell the Queen?" he murmured.

Cleopatra stormed, and wept and pleaded, but at last she saw that she had no choice but to let Antony go. She feared he would not return, but I knew that his love for her was too strong for him to keep away for very long.

\* \* \*

In Rome, Antony was a grizzled lion,

Caesar a cold and haughty eagle,

and Lepidus a crab, scurrying beside them.

They talked behind locked doors, late into the night and standing guard outside, I heard Antony and Caesar raise their voices in anger, while Lepidus twittered and whined.

Antony emerged from the chamber looking tired and worried. He took me aside and said, "I want you to leave for Egypt at once. Tell the Queen that I have made my peace with Caesar."

I frowned: this was good news – yet Antony's face was troubled.

"But the peace came at a price," he went on. "To strengthen the alliance, I must marry Octavia, Caesar's sister. Tell the Queen that the marriage means nothing, and that my love for her is unchanged. I will return to Egypt with Octavia when we have signed a treaty with Pompeius."

Doubts rose in my mind like a flock of crows. All Rome knew how dearly Caesar loved his sister. How long would it be before he discovered that her  marriage to Antony was a sham? It would be all the excuse he needed to declare war and try to seize the whole Empire for himself. And when Cleopatra heard of the marriage, who could tell what she might do? I glimpsed Antony's future, and it was all blood and shadows.

✳ ✳ ✳

I had no flowery words to decorate Antony's message. I spoke out like a soldier, blunt and plain.

Cleopatra's rage was furious. "Tell me that you are lying, or you shall be whipped with wire and boiled in salted water!" she shrieked.

"Madam, I speak the truth," I said. "Antony is married to Octavia." Cleopatra drew a knife; I do not know whether she intended to stab me or herself, for one of her handmaidens snatched the knife away. Cleopatra shook her head, scattering tears that gleamed as they fell. "Then let Egypt sink into the Nile!" she moaned. "Let the sky fall and crush the Earth!"

Egypt did not sink, nor did the sky fall, but one terrible happening led to another.

Before Antony and Octavia were halfway to Egypt, Caesar broke the treaty with Pompeius, defeated him in battle, seized the African provinces and had Lepidus put to death. Antony knew that war was coming, and sent Octavia back to Rome, being too honourable a man to keep her as a hostage.

Once Antony was back in Egypt,
he and Cleopatra joined forces against
Caesar. Though their love remained
strong, some of the fire between them
had dwindled because of Antony's
marriage of convenience.

Antony seemed his old self again, confident and decisive; but also headstrong, as if age had made him stubborn instead of wise. Against all advice, he insisted on a battle at sea, to prevent Caesar from landing his troops.

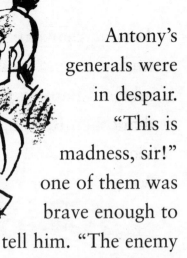

Antony's generals were in despair. "This is madness, sir!" one of them was brave enough to tell him. "The enemy ships greatly outnumber ours. If we lose the fleet, we cannot keep our troops supplied. Fight Caesar on land!"

"Let no man say that Antony feared to face an enemy," Antony replied. "I will meet Caesar at sea!"

Actium, they called that battle. I still
dream of it, and wake up shouting. The
ships fired flaming pitch and sulphur at
one another. Burning men leapt screaming

into the sea and when two ships came
alongside, soldiers from each tried to
board the other, so the decks ran red.

For a time, it seemed that Antony might be victorious; then love betrayed him. Cleopatra sailed out in her barge, thinking that the sight of her would encourage Antony and the Egyptian fleet; but the horror and slaughter of the battle made her order the barge back to harbour.

A Roman galley broke formation to give chase, and Antony turned his ship around to go to Cleopatra's rescue. When the captains of the fleet saw their commander leave the fight, they believed that all was lost, and fled.

After the disaster at Actium, Antony bargained for peace. He offered Caesar his third of the Empire, in return for being allowed to stay in Egypt with the Queen.

Caesar refused: he would make peace with Cleopatra, he said, but only if Antony were executed.

Antony accused Cleopatra of betraying him, out of spite for his marriage to Octavia. Cleopatra was terrified by Antony's fury, and went into hiding.

The generals had their land battle in the end – outside the walls of Alexandria. We fought like heroes, and Caesar's men fell like wheat to the scythe. But even as the celebrations began in Antony's tent, a messenger arrived with grave news. The Egyptian fleet had surrendered; Antony could no longer keep his army fed and armed; the war was lost.

Antony ordered everyone from the tent, except me. When we were alone, he drew his sword and offered it to me, hilt first.

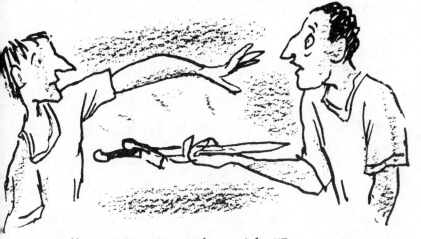

"Kill me, Servius," he said. "I cannot bear to beg Caesar for mercy."

"Sir," I said, "I know where the Queen is hiding. You could be with her in an hour. You could escape to…"

"To live in fear until Caesar hunts us down?" said Antony. "No, Servius. I am finished. Take the sword and end it."

"Not I, sir!" I said. "I would gladly die for you, but I will not do what you ask."

"Then by my own hand be it," said Antony.

He stabbed with both hands, but the point of the sword slipped on his breastbone and ran into his belly. He pulled out the sword and threw it across the tent with a cry of disgust, knowing that his death would be long and painful. Agony drove him to his knees. "Cleopatra!" he gasped. "Take me to her!"

* * *

I do not know how Antony found the
strength to stand, and mount a horse, but
as night fell we rode across the desert to
Cleopatra's hiding place: her own tomb,
built in the shape of a crouching lion with
a man's head. I beat against the doors, my
shouts echoing off the stone, until a slave
answered, and drew back the bolts. Antony
leaned on me, and we staggered inside.

235

The tomb was lit by a hundred oil lamps that shone on the richly decorated walls. Paintings of Egyptian Gods stared down with sightless, animal eyes. Cleopatra was seated on a throne, dressed in her royal robes. A reed basket stood at her feet, and I remember thinking it a poor thing to find in such a place.

Cleopatra saw the blood from Antony's wound, and ran to him. We gently laid him down. Cleopatra sat, and rested his head on her lap.

"I am dying, Egypt," Antony said. "Tell Caesar you had me killed, and make peace with him."

"Never!" said Cleopatra.

Antony's face clenched in pain. "Then add one more kiss to the thousands you have given me," he said.

Cleopatra lowered her head, pressed her lips to Antony's, and he was gone.

"The sun has burned out," Cleopatra whispered. "The world is dark."

Tears clouded
my eyes. I did
not see the
Queen stand,
or reach into
the basket and
take out the small

black snake coiled within it.
When I could see again, she was on her
throne, and the snake's
fangs were sunk deep
in her breast.
"Sweet as perfume!"
she said. "Soft
as air! Oh,
Antony!"

And so her
life ended.

✳ ✳ ✳

And that's my story. It will be told and retold, until time ends. Antony and Cleopatra will always be together, though their beauty and greatness turned to desert dust long ago.

They say that in the East, Emperor Octavius Caesar is worshipped as a God. Well, if Caesar is a God, then let my death come soon, for the world is past my understanding.

But Antony – now there was a man!

*She shall be buried by her Antony.*
*No grave upon the earth shall clip in it*
*A pair so famous.*

Caesar; V.ii.

# Love and Death in
# Antony and Cleopatra

When Mark Antony and Cleopatra meet, they both know that they have found the love of their lives.

Antony is a Roman, a disciplined soldier, and a courageous and brilliant general who rules a third of the Roman Empire. Queen Cleopatra of Egypt is beautiful, stubborn, fiery-tempered and used to having her own way. Yet in spite of their differences, Antony's love for Cleopatra is so strong that he abandons Rome and stays in Egypt, where they live together and have several children.

Then history turns against them. In order to keep the Roman world united, Antony is forced to marry the sister of Octavius Caesar. The marriage is a sham and Antony quickly returns to Egypt, but this gives the ambitious Octavius the excuse he needs to make war and take the whole empire for himself.

Against the advice of his generals, Antony fights the Roman fleet at Actium, where Cleopatra's meddling causes a massive defeat. Antony bungles a suicide attempt and is taken to Cleopatra's hiding place. He dies in her arms.

Antony sacrifices everything for Cleopatra – his reputation, his loyalty to his country, and his life. After he is dead, Octavius offers Cleopatra peace, but she chooses a noble death over a shameful surrender. Cleopatra cannot bear to live without Antony and joins him in death, passing out of history into legend, where her and Antony's love will live for ever.

# Shakespeare and the Globe Theatre

Some of Shakespeare's most famous plays were first performed at the Globe Theatre, which was built on the South Bank of the River Thames in 1599.

Going to the Globe was a different experience from going to the theatre today. The building was roughly circular in shape, but with flat sides: a little like a doughnut crossed with a fifty-pence piece. Because the Globe was an open-air theatre, plays were only put on during daylight hours in spring and summer. People paid a penny to stand in the central space and watch a play, and this part of the audience became known as 'the groundlings' because they stood on the ground. A place in the tiers of seating beneath the thatched roof, where there was a slightly better view and less chance of being rained on, cost extra.

The Elizabethans did not bath very often and the audiences at the Globe were smelly. Fine ladies and gentlemen in the more expensive seats sniffed perfume and bags of sweetly-scented herbs to cover the stink rising from the groundlings.

There were no actresses on the stage; all the female characters in Shakespeare's plays would have been acted by boys, wearing wigs and make-up. Audiences were not well-behaved. People clapped and cheered when their favourite actors came on stage; bad actors were jeered at and sometimes pelted with whatever came to hand.

Most Londoners worked hard to make a living and in their precious free time they liked to be entertained. Shakespeare understood the magic of the theatre so well that today, almost four hundred years after his death, his plays still cast a spell over the thousands of people that go to see them.

*READ ON FOR AN*
*EXTRACT FROM*

# Cast List

### Hermia
In love with Lysander

### Helena
Friend to Hermia
In love with Demetrius

### Demetrius
Betrothed to Hermia

### Lysander
In love with Hermia

Oberon

King of the Fairies

Titania

Queen of the Fairies

Puck

An Elf

Bottom

A Weaver

# The Scene

In and around Athens, Ancient Greece.

# A Midsummer Night's Dream

When the path of true love runs smoothly, the world seems a wonderful place – all bright skies and smiling faces.

Unfortunately, true love has a habit of wandering off the path and getting lost, and when that happens people's lives get lost too, in a tangle of misery.

Take the love
of Duke Theseus
of Athens and
Hippolyta, Queen
of the Amazons, for
instance. They were to
be married, and their happiness spread
through the whole of Athens. People had
decorated their houses with flowers, and
left lamps burning in their windows at
night, so that the streets twinkled like a

city of stars. Everybody
was joyful and excited
as they prepared to
celebrate the Duke's
wedding day.
Well, almost
everybody…

* * *

252

On the day before the royal wedding, two friends met by chance in the market square: golden-haired Hermia, and black-haired Helena, both beautiful and both with secrets that made their hearts ache.

For a while, the two friends chatted about nothing in particular. Then Helena noticed a look in Hermia's deep blue eyes that made her ask, "Is everything all right, Hermia?"

Hermia looked so sad and serious.

"I am to marry Demetrius tomorrow," she replied.

"Demetrius!" said Helena softly. Now her heart was aching worse than ever. Night after night she had cried herself to sleep, whispering Demetrius's name, knowing that her love for him was hopeless.  Many years ago the families of Hermia and Demetrius had agreed that, when they were of age, their daughter and son should marry. "You must be the happiest young woman in Athens!" sighed Helena.

"I've never been so miserable in my life!" Hermia declared. "You see, I don't love Demetrius."

"You don't?" cried Helena, amazed.

Read

## A MIDSUMMER NIGHT'S DREAM

and more Shakespeare classics in

More Shakespeare Stories